HOMETOWN
NEW ZEALAND

HOMETOWN NEW ZEALAND

PHOTOGRAPHS BY DEREK SMITH

craig potton publishing

What The Gas Man Saw

'This'll do till a real job comes up,' I thought, and took the card to the counter. *Meter reader wanted for six weeks' work.* Must be fit and unafraid of dogs. It was April 1981 and I had just returned from four months of picking and stacking tobacco at Woodstock, in the stunningly beautiful Motueka River valley. It was good to get back into Auckland's urban fizz but I had no idea what my next job would be. I was directed for my interview to the Auckland Gas Company's main office in Wyndham Street and met my prospective boss, Paul, a flamboyant ex-teacher, who obviously had dreams beyond being a meter-reading coordinator. The meter reader I was to replace was suffering from a nervous disorder and was on six weeks' leave – a warning that went foolishly unheeded. Paul obviously favoured his friends when it came to choosing his workforce, which consisted of an eclectic mix of older career meter readers in the traditional Public Service mould, and a group of frustrated academics who needed an income to support their artistic strivings. I was issued with my Swanndri, blue polyester pants and clipboard and sent into the urban morass on a bright yellow Honda 125.

The first day was a revelation. I was shown the ropes by a retiring meter reader and after a 15-minute apprenticeship was sent off down Dominion Road. After finishing my block in about three hours, I returned to my mentor for more work. 'That's it,' he said. 'You can bugger off now.' It was barely midday and I had finished my round. Bloody marvellous. I could easily get used to this. And I did.

The sense of purpose was questionable but the sense of liberty was unique. Each day of issued work was generally completed well within five hours, and provided that the work was done that day it could be distributed across the eight hours. Any breaks were unofficially at my discretion. No one was waiting at their letterboxes for the meter reader to call and the film festivals beckoned. The only negative was having to deal with the consequences of disclosing my profession at social gatherings. But usually after educating people as to the real nature of the work, they would hassle me for Paul's phone number.

Auckland is made up of dozens of suburban territories and this job required me to become intimate with all of them. I grew up in the sixties and seventies among the pohutukawa and sandstone cliffs, placid beaches and baches of seaside suburbia in the East Coast Bays. It was considered recklessly adventurous to cross the harbour bridge. The wide, red-chip paths and ancient wooden villas of Ponsonby and Grey Lynn were hugely exotic. I was already taking a serious interest in photography at this time and was reading and viewing all I could on the subject. I was at an age of questioning the sense of purpose in my life. Having no pressure at all from parents or peers, I decided that photography was a pursuit of substance. It seemed that if a personal space is threatened either through fire, flood or invasion, the most treasured possessions were almost always personal photographs. Taking that idea a little further, images of our social environment may be considered a valuable contribution to our society as a whole. A major influence was Janet Malcolm's 1980 book of illustrated essays on photography, *Diana and Nikon*, which introduced me to the stunning clarity of Edward Weston's vision, the social documentary work of Walker Evans and the enigmatic and strangely compelling colour work of William Eggleston (albeit reproduced in black and white). I was always attracted to the creative rendering of the utterly ordinary and was totally immersed in my favourite raw material through the nature of my new job. I took my camera with me to work every day and began to see aesthetic worth everywhere. New environments are always visually stimulating, but through viewing the historical work of Walker Evans and Les Cleveland, I also began to recognise our place in time as being relatively transient and important to document.

Robin Morrison's iconic and influential *The South Island of New Zealand from the Road* (1981) had just been published and validated the use of colour in serious work. I made efforts to record anything that might represent any current visual fashion in its contemporary context. Suddenly my job had a great sense of purpose and I wanted more than six weeks. When the reader I replaced was due to return, Paul managed to create a new reading position for me as a 'relief' reader, which soon became permanent. I have always enjoyed exploring and discovering, and this was the perfect way to indulge my curiosity and earn a living wage. This work took me intimately through every social aspect of the city. It required us to enter every reticulated property and, in many cases, private living areas where the meters were inside. Reading rounds were often rotated, enabling us to become familiar with the entire city. We were issued with a bunch of between 20 and 40 keys daily to gain access to meters when property owners were absent. I soon gained a unique insight into a broad cross-section of our community, and I was utterly fascinated by it – more anthropologically than voyeuristically. Meters were generally located in kitchens or cupboards or basements or wherever people were least likely to see them. My social impressions of the city soon had far greater dimension. It was totally inappropriate for me to photograph inside private property and I never did, but I photographed as much as I could from the street. I had the perfect opportunity to document from a personal perspective and the financial means to do it.

My afternoons were relatively free and I would often spend hours in the Elam art school library, which had an extensive photographic reference section. In an environment known for its expressive clothing, I felt a little obvious in my tacky Swanndri and blue polyester pants, but fortunately my enforced dress sensibility never caught on with the students. I made an ally of John B. Turner, the senior photography lecturer, who strongly supported the work I was doing and encouraged my access to the library's material. I joined PhotoForum and enjoyed the company and influence of other photographers.

The six-week schedule took in the entire urban area from Wiri to Castor Bay, and every suburb had a distinct character. This was often reflected in the behaviour of the dogs, which determined my daily adrenaline input. Anxious times were had in the state housing areas where the dogs were wild and free and could sense your vulnerability. Often roaming in packs in the open neighbourhoods, they made you wish you were inside, stacking supermarket shelves. But the stress out there was of the fight or flight variety and once you survived the day, you could leave it behind. Primal instincts were tested constantly, first by the harrowing dance through heavy Auckland traffic on seriously underpowered motorcycles, followed by the daily confrontation with beasts unknown. But the whole experience, combined with the constantly changing visual input, was becoming increasingly addictive. Meter reading was the most sensually exciting, socially educating and uncommonly liberal job I had ever had. And no one else seemed to know.

By now, Paul had enlisted a fascinating crew of individuals comprising painters, writers, musicians and philosophers – all of whom relished the freedom, the exercise, the insight and the regular income that the job offered. A line-up of bright red and yellow Hondas soon congested the entrance to the local coffee house in Wyndham Street every morning, and debate would rage from the then-current dire nuclear situation, the elation and then confusion over the new Labour government, to the latest Jim Jarmusch offering. We were all soon promoted to Suzuki 250s, which finally gave us half a chance on the motorways. Except

for one, which we christened 'Certain Death' due to its primitive front drum brake. It was instant hero status for anyone who volunteered to go out on Certain Death after a decent shower of rain.

At the end of every month we would all be called upon to read the commercial customers, which took us to every reticulated business in the city from the Regent Hotel to the Pink Pussycat to the Southdown Freezing Works and beyond. It was a fascinating insight into the working lives of much of the population. Generally the meters were located behind the public façade, and often in the engine room of large businesses where the human grind was openly evident. Glenn Busch's wonderful photographic survey *Working Men* (1986) was particularly relevant in my experience of these conditions.

All of us were influenced on some level by the experiences that the work offered and I'm sure it affected our relationship with the greater Auckland area in a profound sense. It was hard to imagine a job that required such intimate involvement with the physical and social characteristics of a major city. By its nature, this relationship was totally democratic. We were required to work in every social environment, in all weather and seasonal conditions and on motorcycles – at a time when the physical and political landscape of the city was being constantly transformed. This was a truly exciting job in the most primal sense possible.

Many of the photographers whose work I most admired were using medium- or large-format equipment for precise rendering of detail and greater colour control. I had to have the quality, but needed portability, so I purchased a near-new Mamiya 645 from a pharmacy in Mangere. What a wonderful tool this proved to be. Sally Eauclaire had just published *The New Colour Photography* (1981), containing what I considered the most insightful writings I had yet read on the subject and this soon became my bible. The colonial rawness and commercial evidence of the American social landscape had its parallels here and I identified strongly with the commentary that some of the New Colour photographers were expressing. Many New Zealanders rightly viewed their country as though in a travel brochure, but my intense daily visual involvement with the urban 'everyday' showed me the unique beauty and social and personal metaphor that can exist in the most seemingly mundane scene. From the perspective of personal expression, I became excited by the intellectual quality of form and the emotional expression of colour. I soon found that the best images combined both of these aspects in a picture that was also motivated by a social response. Colour was largely determined by light quality, and for my language this meant the best light was autumn and winter, preferably with a cloudless sky leaving the light clear and golden. One cloud in a vast winter sky could change the nature of the sunlight like a white diffuser.

Many of my photographs were taken from a documentary perspective because I was there, basically, but occasionally all the elements were right for a satisfyingly expressive image and this was magic. *Metro* magazine published a selection in 1983 that was well received. I had been riding motorcycles since I was 15 and I was thoroughly enjoying the daily combat on the suburban streets. For a while I also took on courier work in the afternoons on my own bike, and at one stage also delivered pizzas by motorcycle at night. A totally different city was revealed and not one that I was drawn to photograph. Very good money, but 12–14 hours daily on motorcycles on Auckland streets pushed the boundaries a little and after a few scary incidents, I abandoned my other jobs and happily settled for the one income.

Every Christmas I would jaunt down to the South Island on my motorcycle to visit my parents who had left Auckland in 1980 and settled in Motueka. This gave me a wonderful opportunity to document the small North Island townships that I passed through on the way. I love the Nelson region and soon felt the need to spend some serious time in the area to build up a body of work. I left Auckland in 1988 with a carload of possessions and set myself up in a pickers' bach in Lower Moutere. Within a month, a meter-reading job was advertised with Tasman Energy and I managed to secure it. It was good fortune, really – these jobs seldom become available and this one only came up due to a retirement. The work was totally different in nature to my Auckland job, but equally fascinating. I was issued with a small car and the reading area covered the entire northwestern section of the South Island from Farewell Spit to Springs Junction and everything in between, apart from Nelson City which had its own readers. I thought I would miss the visual excitement of Auckland's frenetic urban landscape but soon found endless stimulation with the undiscovered form, colour and social character of the farms, orchards and small towns of the region. We were required to read the meters of every electrical connection in the area. This took us to every pumpshed, shearing shed, forestry lookout, farmhouse, orchard, hop and tobacco kiln and more. We rotated our rounds so everyone had some idea where these connections were. The meter readers here were of an entirely different social mould to those in Auckland – they were all locals who had been enjoying the job for years and had many colourful stories of meter-reading folklore.

Nelson light was cuttingly clear and inspiring, particularly during autumn and winter. Colours were vivid and rich. The climate was distinctly seasonal and invigorating: hot, dry summers, wildly colourful autumns and cool, crisp and calm winters, almost always uncannily sunny. The previously bewildering work of Toss Woollaston began to make a lot more sense after spending several summers here. There is a distinct purity in the people, the climate and the environment, that was in graphic contrast to the commercially driven and semi-polluted (socially and physically) watery isthmus of Auckland. This environment also presented a new variety of hazards, which I was soon to discover. Often the pumpsheds were in fenced paddocks, and rutting stags on deer farms made the rotties and pit bulls of Mangere and Otara seem like lap dogs. Many electric fences made their deterrent qualities well felt. I think some farmers deliberately put their most difficult bulls in the same paddocks as the pumpsheds for a spot of entertainment when the meter reader arrived. Some problems were self-imposed, such as trying to cross unknown fords in a Mitsubishi Mirage and suddenly finding water up to the top of the gear lever inside the car, which was slowly sliding downstream. The country dogs were a welcome relief. In total contrast to many urban dogs, the working dogs here were pleased and excited to receive visitors and packs of six or more would happily welcome the meter reader when they spotted the car approaching. The meter location details were often fundamental and we required highly developed orienteering skills to locate some of the connections. 'Just follow the wires' was the best advice but there would always be a farm or two with underground reticulation. It was great fun and always interesting.

I was reading Julie Riley's *Men Alone* (1990) and discovered a number of the book's subjects and others like them living in the most remote parts of the Golden Bay and Buller regions. Most were happy to have a yarn and I always treasured my time with them. Many of the farmhouses were vacated during the day as the inhabitants attended to chores, and a common instruction on the meter-reading sheets was 'door open, go in' – unheard of in Auckland. Rural realities were an eye opener for me. Often worksheds were surrounded by animal skins and the casualties of the lambing season, which contrasted markedly with the lush growth of new spring grass. One particular forestry lookout meter required 48 stops and starts if all 12 gates on the access road happened to be closed during lambing. I eventually concluded that if I was to do anything with these rapidly amassing images (over thirty thousand at this stage), I ought to have some form of formal photographic tuition to lend some public credibility to my passion.

In 1991, I applied for and was accepted into Wellington Polytechnic's professional photography course and soon realised that professional photography had very little to do with what I was trying to express. But the star student on the course, Maclean Barker, was stunningly lovely and so I convinced myself to stay if only for an excuse to be near her. The head tutor, Tony Whincup, was sympathetic and soon became aware of what I needed to do, giving me great freedom to document the unique and colourful Wellington urban landscape. Maclean and I soon grew very close and so began another branch of my life's meaning.

After the course was completed, I had the amazingly good fortune to land another meter-reading job in central Wellington. The conditions were similar to my previous work, enabling me to become intimately involved with the very physical and visual nature of this hugely characterful city. Much has been published about Wellington and its endless visual inspiration and I felt it challenging to add anything that hadn't already been represented. Again, the meter-reading work was done on motorcycles, and it soon became evident that the biggest hazard here was surviving a day of a cuttingly icy southerly storm without ending up horizontal or having completely seized limbs by the end of it. Walking up and down 137 steps to a domestic property and repeating the process for the next house wasn't a lot of fun either. Sleep came easy at the end of a Roseneath day. It was always amusing to see the conscientious office dwellers sweating away on treadmills at the gym knowing that I had already done my 15 kilometres that day, out in the fresh air, and had been paid for it, too. The tragedy was, I was still overweight after 15 years of this effort – with marvellous thighs, though.

While in Wellington, I was lucky enough to chat on occasions with Bill Main, one of the country's greatest photographic enthusiasts. When showing him some of my latest graphic work he commented: 'Very nice but these could have been taken anywhere and at any time.' Those words dictated the philosophy that has remained with me since. Composition, light and colour needed to be combined with a sense of time and place for the images to have their greatest resonance.

Around this time, Kim Hill, our most astute radio broadcaster, had secured a position as the host of Nine To Noon on National Radio. This meant that from then on, a discreet AM radio with earbuds became a compulsory part of the meter-reader's uniform.

After Maclean had finished her studies (she did a further year at polytech exploring and developing her own photographic voice), we decided to retreat to the sheltered embrace of Motueka. Maclean became a pillar of the local community by revitalising the local museum, of which she remained the manager and curator for the following five years. After a short stint on the apples, another meter-reading job became available to me, this time in the previously unexplored urban Nelson area. Back to the rich, clear light and calm sunny days. This was possibly the least inspiring meter-reading stint. There were no rural areas this time and Wellington is a hard act to follow for urban landscape. Still, it was a tolerable job and gave us security while we brought up our beautiful son, Oscar.

The government's power reforms were now having a serious effect on the nature of the job. The company I worked for was passed through the hands of four different electricity retailers in the following eight years, all with very different company cultures, which was very unsettling for workers and customers alike. Company accountants with no idea of the physical reality of the job had scrutinised the role of the relatively unskilled meter reader via computer printouts and decided that high output and high staff turnover were more important than a regular face at the door, and soon the job lost all of its endearing qualities. We were now power walking in the Nelson hills for eight hours a day and it soon became totally exhausting. My knees and ankles were rapidly deteriorating and I had no time to take pictures or talk with customers. It had become another production-line job. It was time to save my body and soul and move on.

Of all the urban environments in this amazing country of ours, Dunedin offers the most historically interesting. It was a wealthy town when much of its urban landscape was formed, giving it a unique architectural heritage that, fortunately, it hasn't had the money or will since to destroy. I was fascinated by its quirky charm on my previous visits and I had always wanted an excuse to spend a good deal of time there and become familiar with the visual nature of the city and the region. It seemed that much of the domestic architecture turned to red brick from Timaru south and this gave the urban landscape a distinct character in a New Zealand context. The southerly nature of the city gave the winter light a surreal quality that accentuated the beauty of the unique forms that reflected it. We were at a stage to entertain a change after spending eight years in Motueka and although life there was idyllic in many respects, it felt to me a little like having your pudding before the main course. We were ready for the challenges of the Deep South.

Shortly after moving down, and not having my previous good luck with finding meter-reading work, I joined, on a voluntary basis, the Southern Heritage Trust, which was set up by the tirelessly enthusiastic Ann Barsby to promote the many heritage aspects of the region. This gave me access as an official photographer to many of the historical sites in Otago and an opportunity to document this endlessly inspiring city. Maclean soon found a rewarding position as the curator at Larnach Castle and Oscar happily plugged into all the new-found stimulus of this energetic university town.

After several years of visual immersion, I accumulated a large number of images of Dunedin city and the Otago region that were used by the Southern Heritage and Historic Places trusts, and gave my photographic wanderings a sense of purpose. We gained so much more insight into New Zealand from this very important region through both the landscape and heritage perspectives. But it was quite nippy and so we thought a spell in warmer territory might be in order. We always knew that we would finally settle in the Nelson region, which really is our spiritual home, so we agreed to one last good session in the North Island. The region that appealed to us most in our younger days was the Coromandel. It had a stunning coastline and was on the social fringe, at least when we knew it in the seventies. We took an exploratory journey to check which areas suited us and had our eyes well opened to the changes that had altered the whole feel of the place. Thames was still a charming town and really appealed to us, but the east coast had a special relationship with the Pacific Ocean so we searched for an area that suited us but, more importantly, that we could afford. All

of the beach areas had now become the weekend playground of wealthy Aucklanders. It was no longer an isolated haven with dodgy access and we were a bit disillusioned with our options. Waihi Beach had managed to avoid major redevelopment and still retained a certain amount of traditional Kiwi seaside charm, so we bought a small block with a sixties farmhouse, just back from the beach and settled into a spot of rural seaside bliss. It was a great spot to explore the North Island from – an easy drive to Auckland and Northland and handy to the central plateau, Tauranga and, of course, the Coromandel Peninsula.

Although bereft of the heritage aspects of the Deep South, the seaside bach culture beckoned to be photographed before it was too late. The physical beauty of the area is astonishing but I have avoided pointing my camera at it because a photograph never seems to do justice to the feel of being there. I preferred to concentrate on bringing attention to scenes that would otherwise go unnoticed or that I felt required documenting. To start with I earned a living mowing lawns for absent property owners but then I stumbled upon the most astounding meter-reading job of my career. Property maintenance was a bit spasmodic during the winter months when grass growth slowed and we needed a more regular income, and so I made myself available to a nationwide meter-reading company based in Hamilton as a relief reader in the Coromandel region. During my interview, Mark, my new boss, and an amazing individual, asked if I would mind a bit of travelling to fill in when other readers were off. 'Sounds OK to me,' I said, and so began seven years (so far) of a remarkable adventure.

I love the excitement of travel and the wonderful aspect of meter reading is that your destinations are beyond your control and as in adventure travel anywhere, the unplanned is the most energising aspect. Each day was totally determined by who phoned in sick or who was on leave and so I would look at my handheld computer that morning and find that I was off to Kaitaia for a week or Wellington for two or anywhere in between (often Rotorua, Taupo, Napier, Auckland or the Waikato and, of course, every nook and cranny of the Coromandel region). Maclean was very understanding and knew that I would return with a new harvest of images. I was fed and motelled courtesy of the company and every day was different and very exciting. We all pass through these regions in our local travels but meter reading got me involved with the essence of every aspect of these towns and regions (much of the work was rural) and a chance to chat with the locals from nearly every corner of the island. The work would take me on charter boats to the grid-fed islands in the Bay of Islands to the most remote parts of Tuhoe territory in the central North Island. It really was like being a part of one long and exciting 'fly on the wall' documentary. It was exhausting work with a lot of 10–12-hour days driving in a basic 4WD Daihatsu Terios, but it gave me a unique opportunity to immerse myself in and document the country I love. As a photographer (or more accurately, a chronicler), I could not have wished for a better opportunity to do what I needed to do. It was a true adventure and every day was different. I felt solidly bonded to the country I love.

By now, Oscar was approaching teenhood and had quite an interesting head on his shoulders, and it became obvious to us that he needed a little more stimulation than Waihi or the beach could offer. We had always intended to eventually settle in Nelson and so we brought our plans forward to meet his needs. We scouted about for a suitable house and fell for one before selling our own. Scary financing and several months of urgent marketing saw us finally all settle in the Brook area of Nelson. Oscar would get the progressive environment he needed at Nayland College and Maclean worked first at the Nelson Public Library and then at the legendary Page and Blackmore bookstore. Initially, there was no regular meter-reading work in the Nelson region and so I was assigned as a relief reader in Central Otago, Southland and the West Coast, which was too good for words. After a while, more work became available locally and I read meters in the region from Blenheim to Collingwood and down to Hokitika. After four fascinating years here, Oscar was ready to further his education at Otago University, which placed us in the very liberating position of having no real need for a permanent home. We took advantage of this and sold the house, bought a very comfortable caravan, and are now travelling the country with no real plans other than to absorb and photograph as much as possible. Maclean now has the time to focus on her interpretative photographic work and I am still able to pick up relief meter reading around the country as well as selling pictures through the many markets, which manages to pay the vastly reduced bills. Look out for us in a town near you!

Derek Smith, 2014

RED & YELLOW

Napier, 1985

Lyall Bay, Wellington, 1991

Wellington, 1991

Wellington, 1991

Nelson, 2011

Raetihi, 1986

Island Bay, Wellington, 1991

South coast, Wellington, 1992

Blenheim, 2011

Kaiteriteri, 2012

Bluff, 2010

Green Island, Dunedin, 2003

Miramar, Wellington, 1991

Mount Victoria, Wellington, 1991

Wellington, 1992

Kilbirnie, Wellington, 1991

Westport, 1982

Dunedin, 2003

Richmond, 1988

Wellington, 1992

Kaikoura, 2013

Lyall Bay, Wellington, 1992

Dunedin, 2004

Ponsonby, Auckland, 2006

Blenheim, 2011

Wellington, 1991

Dunedin, 2004

Dunedin, 2004

Ranfurly, 2003

Greymouth, 2012

Tadmor, Tasman, 1988

Oamaru, 2003

Nelson, 2012

Blenheim, 2012

Foxton, 2004

Nelson, 2012

Westport, 2012

Westport, 2012

Dunedin, 2003

Dunedin, 2004

Wellington, 1992

Karitane, 2003

Island Bay, Wellington, 1991

Lyall Bay, Wellington, 1992

Nelson, 1988

Raetihi, 1986

Motueka, 2013

Waihi Beach, 2007

Ravensbourne, Dunedin, 2002

Newtown, Wellington, 1991

Putaruru, 1989

Whiritoa, Coromandel Peninsula, 2008

WHITE

Nelson, 2012

Kaiteriteri, 1982

Reefton, 2012

Reefton, 2012

Cambridge, 2008

Napier, 1982

Motueka, 1989

Wellington, 1991

Takapau, 1992

Aro Valley, Wellington, 1991

Coromandel Peninsula, 2008

Waikato, 2008

Andersons Bay, Dunedin, 2004

Nelson, 1982

Alexandra, 2002

Motueka, 1989

Dannevirke, 1989

Blenheim, 1983

Tuatapere, 2010

Nightcaps, 2010

Titahi Bay, Wellington, 1991

Rawene, Hokianga, 1989

Napier, 1989

Dannevirke, 1995

BLUE & GREEN

Wellington, 2005

Wellington, 2005

Napier, 1992

Napier, 1992

Whangamata, 2012

Picton, 2012

Motueka, 1989

Albany, 1983

Nelson, 2012

Auckland, 1983

Tasman, 2012

Wakefield, Tasman, 1988

Te Aroha, 2008

Te Aroha, 2008

Wellington, 1992

Blenheim, 2011

Motueka, 2012

Nelson, 2005

Taranaki, 2007

Island Bay, Wellington, 1991

Wellington, 1991

Thames, 1983

Hokitika, 1998

Nelson, 1989

Nelson, 2012

Auckland, 1982

Granity, West Coast, 2012

Moutere, Tasman, 2012

Wellington, 2004

Taihape, 2009

Wakefield, Tasman, 1988

Greymouth, 2013

Wellington, 1991

Wellington, 1991

Wellington, 1991

Greymouth, 2013

Whangamata, 2008

Whiritoa, Coromandel Peninsula, 2008

Tasman, 1989

Northland, 2009

Masterton, 1989

Masterton, 1989

Gore, 2010

Patea, Taranaki, 1984

Motueka, 2012

Whangarei, 2009

Reefton, 2013

Lumsden, 2002

Kaiaua, Firth of Thames, 2008

Thames coast, 2008

Published in 2014
Craig Potton Publishing, 98 Vickerman Street, PO Box 555, Nelson, New Zealand
www.craigpotton.co.nz

© Photography: Derek Smith

ISBN 978-1-927213-11-7

Printed in China by Midas Printing International Ltd